Basil the Brilliant!

Who has not heard of Sherlock Holmes? Men hail him as the master detective of all time.

Mice proudly hail their own super-sleuth, Basil of Baker Street. No case is too difficult or too dangerous for this daring detective. . . .

I am David Q. Dawson, and Basil and I lodge at Baker Street, which is also the address of Mr. Sherlock Holmes and Dr. John H. Watson. The men dwell abovestairs and the mice belowstairs.

My friend learns his detective lore by listening at his hero's feet when scientific sleuthing is discussed. He takes many notes in short-paw, hidden behind a chair leg.

To give you an example of my friend's genius, I shall describe how he solved a case in a few short hours, a case that had baffled Mouseland Yard detectives for weeks . . .

BASIL

IN MEXICO

BASIL
IN MEXICO

❧❂❧

A BASIL OF BAKER STREET MYSTERY

BY EVE TITUS

ILLUSTRATED BY
PAUL GALDONE

AN ARCHWAY PAPERBACK
Published by POCKET BOOKS • NEW YORK

An Archway Paperback published by
POCKET BOOKS, a division of Simon & Schuster, Inc.
1230 Avenue of the Americas, New York, N.Y. 10020

Published by arrangement with McGraw-Hill Book Company
Library of Congress Catalog Card Number: 75-10827

ISBN: 0-671-55718-1

First Pocket Books printing August, 1977

10 9 8 7 6 5 4 3

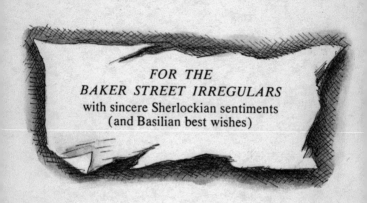

FOR THE
BAKER STREET IRREGULARS
with sincere Sherlockian sentiments
(and Basilian best wishes)

CAST OF CHARACTERS

BASIL	*an English mouse detective*
DR. DAWSON	*his friend and associate*
MRS. JUDSON	*their mousekeeper*
INSPECTOR HOLLYER	*a Mouseland Yard detective*
DR. RICHARDSON	*a mouse dentist*
SIMONE	*his wife*
PROFESSOR RATIGAN	*arch villain*
MARLANE	*a liberated female mouse*
DIEGO NOVATO	*her husband*
ROBERT JOSTES	*an American artist*
CAPTAIN RYDER	*a British seamouse*
LUIS GODOY	*a museum curator*
JULIO SALDAÑA	*a museum director*
PILÁR	*a nosey file clerk*
PABLO	*a workmouse*
ROMANO	*a museum guard*
LUTHER NORRIS	*a bookmouse*
GENERAL SIERRA	*a military mouse*
EL BRUTO	*a dictator*

SIR JOHN HATHAWAY — *British mouse ambassador*

LADY PAULA — *his wife*

CARMENCITA — *a friendly Mexican burro*

PEPITO — *her young nephew*

LORD ADRIAN

MAHARAJAH OF BENGISTAN

BOB HAHN

FRANK REILLY — *Mouse Mountaineers (alphabetically)*

YOUNG RICHARD

VINCENZO STARRETTI

DR. JULIAN WOLFF

And introducing:

THE PANADERO STREET IRREGULARS
(seven young Mexican mice)

GANGSTER MICE

BRITISH SEAMICE

MEXICAN MICE

(and a cast of thousands!)

CONTENTS

1

Basil the Brilliant

Who has not heard of Sherlock Holmes? Men hail him as the master detective of all time.

Mice proudly hail their own super-sleuth, Basil of Baker Street. No case is too difficult or too dangerous for this daring detective, and criminals cringe at the sound of his name.

I am Dr. David Q. Dawson, and Basil and I lodge at Baker Street, number 221,B, which is also the address of Mr. Sherlock Holmes and Dr. John H. Watson. The men dwell abovestairs and the mice belowstairs, in the cellar community of Holmestead, so named by Basil.

My friend learns his detective lore by listening at his hero's feet when scientific sleuthing is discussed. He takes many notes in shortpaw, hidden behind a chair leg. You may ask —does Sherlock spy him? I think he does, and is charmed by his wee imitator in the deerstalker cap.

To give you an example of my friend's genius, I shall describe how he solved a case in a few short hours, a case that had baffled Mouseland Yard detectives for weeks.

On a crisp October morning in the year 1894 Mrs. Judson served our breakfast. We were to sail at midnight on a secret mission to Mexico.

Basil had a second helping of cheese soufflé.

"My dear mousekeeper," said he, "tomorrow we breakfast at sea. We'll miss your excellent cooking, and your good self as well."

"Sure, and I'll be missing ye both. The Mexican mouse president himself wrote the letter sending for ye. 'Tis a great honor, Mr. Basil!''

Nodding, he scanned the *Mouse Times*.

''Dawson, the Case of the Counterfeit Cheese is still unsolved! Hundreds of mice with broken teeth crowd into dentists' waiting rooms. The fake cheeses look and smell like

real cheeses. Mice sniff them in dark passage-ways and gnaw away. Their reward? The ghastly sound of breaking teeth! There are no clues. Policemice remove the counterfeits, but others appear. Do you recall the Case of the Lost Colony, and the golden hill of cheese with a deadly mousetrap concealed inside?''

I shuddered. "But for your warning, I'd have perished! That evil device was invented by Professor Ratigan, leader of London's mouse underworld. Is this another of his schemes? However, it seems to me that only dentists would profit. I saw my dentist last week. Dr. Tuchman's office was jammed! I joked, told him he'd make millions, but he didn't even smile, and his paws kept twitching and trembling."

"Hmmm. Mrs. Judson, what of your dentist?"

"Mr. Basil, mine wasn't happy about the crowds of patients, either. And, if you'll excuse the expression, he was as nervous as a cat!"

My friend looked thoughtful. "My own dentist, Dr. Richardson, is the happy-go-lucky type, but yesterday he was as jumpy as a kangaroo. His paws shook so much that I feared he'd fill the wrong tooth! One nervous dentist might be a coincidence, but—*three?* Dawson, there must be a reason!"

He leaped up. "By Jove! Can it be that—"

4

There was a knock at the door. Mrs. Judson admitted Inspector Hollyer, of the Yard.

"Basil, we need your help! Superintendent Bigelow asks you to delay your departure and stay to solve the Case of the Counterfeit Cheese."

"Postpone my mission to Mexico? Impossible! However, the case interests me. I'll do my best to solve it by dark and still make that midnight sailing. Tell me all you know, Inspector."

2

The Case of the Counterfeit Cheese

Hollyer had nothing new to report, except that Mouseland Yard detectives had questioned every mouse dentist in London, thirty-two in number.

"They were all nervous," he told us. "We decided this was due to long hours of overwork, fixing broken teeth far into the night."

"Overwork? Stuff and nonsense!" cried Basil. "There's more to it than that. Dawson, kindly pass me the London Mouse Dental Directory."

I fetched the volume from the shelf, and he skimmed the pages, mumbling to himself.

"Hmmm. Richardson, Stanley. Schooling: Spring View, Brierley Preparatory, Rodental College. Married Simone Vernet, son Alex at Brierley. Tuchman, Bernard. Same schools, son Adam at Brierley. St. Clair, N., Trevor, V., Windibank, J. Hmmm. All have sons at Brierley."

He snapped the book shut. "Hollyer, tell Superintendent Bigelow that I have a clue in the Counterfeit Cheese Case. It's important that I see my dentist at once. Come along, Dawson!"

We saw Dr. Richardson in his private office.

Basil wasted no words. "You are being terrorized, and I know why. In heaven's name, speak!"

Richardson hung his head. "Alas, I dare not!"

At that moment his wife entered, crying, *"Cheri, cheri!* Is there any news of our son?"

"Simone, say no more!" warned the dentist.

8

Turning, she saw Basil, and her eyes lit up.

"*M'sieu* Basil, you are our one hope! Only you can outwit the evil Professor Ratigan. I'll stay silent no longer, but will reveal everything. Only the sons of London mouse dentists are accepted at Brierley School. Every October the school closes, and the students and a guide go off on a camping and cycling tour. They write home each day, but this year four days passed with no mail. The lads start by riding through the mouse town of Brierley Glen. The mayor told us they hadn't been seen! Worried, we parents decided to tell the police the next day. And then—"

She trembled. "That very night Stanley and I awoke to see the Professor at our bedside.

"He boasted, 'I invented the fake cheeses, so the money for fixing broken teeth belongs to me. My gangs will collect from now on. Tell the police, or that busybody, Basil of Baker Street, and you'll never see your sons again!'

"Then he was gone! Gangsters come daily to collect. When dentists ask about their children, the scoundrels sneer. Please help us!"

Basil patted her paw. "Madame, do not despair! They shall be saved! We must leave you now."

We rushed along the London streets. The huge, hurrying feet of humans loomed like marching monsters. City mice risk death by squashing far too often, and we are ever watchful. At Charing Cross Station Basil stole aboard a people's train for Chatham. From there he planned to hike to the mouse town of Brierley Glen.

I went home. Basil returned at nine that night. Then Hollyer arrived, happily excited.

"Superintendent Bigelow thanks you, sir! After you telephoned the location of the counterfeit cheese factory, we raided it, and made some arrests, but Ratigan and his chief aides escaped. However, we closed down the factory."

"Good work!" said Basil. "Bigelow, wise as a judge, is bound to promote you. Now I'll

tell you my part in the affair. In Brierley Glen I rented a bicycle, and rode to Brierley School. Not a soul was in sight—I was the solitary cyclist. The buildings were set back from the road, except for the bicycle shed, just inside the front gates. I squeezed under and

entered the shed. The bicycles were grimy and dusty, tumbled together in wild disorder, and tossed every which way. I'd found my final clue!"

"Enlighten us," begged Hollyer. "What clue?"

"Elementary, my dear mice! Boys, be they mouse or human, may neglect their clothes, their rooms, their books. Necks may go unwashed, bodies unbathed, but never do they neglect their beloved bicycles. They rub,

scrub, and polish for hours, until the things sparkle like the crown jewels!

"Clearly, no boys had flung the bicycles inside—gangsters had! With a good food supply, what better hideaway than the deserted school? I rode back, alerted the town police-mice, and we moved in. Outnumbered, the gang gave up. They'd ambushed the lads and forced them back to the school."

Hollyer beamed. "You're brilliant, sir! Good luck on your secret mission to Mexico!"

"A secret even to me," said Basil. "The hour grows late, Dawson. We'd best depart."

Outside we found thirty-two thankful dentists who paid Basil a princely fee, promised us free dental care forever, and waved as we dashed down Baker Street in the swirling fog.

Our destination—a people's ship bound for Mexico!

3

On the High Seas

The *Ruth Low* was a medium-sized cargo vessel. Watching our chance, we stole up the gangway, unobserved by the brawny men loading the ship.

We scurried to the ship's hold, into a corner where the men seldom went. The ship's mice had built comfortable quarters there, on a high shelf. Shown to our stateroom, we slept well.

Basil awakened me early. "Captain's compliments, Dawson. We're to sit at his table."

A surprise awaited us—the captain was Cecil Ryder, once our classmate at Ratcliffe College.

Beside Basil sat a lovely lady mouse, with large, lustrous eyes and the velvety smooth fur typical of English females. She was introduced as Marlane, the wife of Mexico's mouse president.

Basil's eyes twinkled. "Let me see—you are a writer, born in Mexico of British parents, and speak Spanish and English equally well. Diego Novato, your husband, led the revolt against the cruel dictator, *El Bruto*. Your husband was then elected president, and *El Bruto* was exiled."

"Amazing, Basil! What else do you know?"

"That you're not on this ship by chance, but with a purpose—to tell me all about my mission."

She nodded. "The messenger who delivered your letter from Mexico told me on what ship you'd sail. I've been rushing around Europe, researching my next book, *Famous Female Mice,* and prefer to relax awhile. We'll

16

be at sea a couple of weeks—may I go into detail later on?''

"I'll wait, Marlane, but only if you promise to help us master the Spanish language."

She agreed, and we talked of other things.

Ryder said that mouse captains and their crews sailed twice a year on people's ships, to learn more by watching men navigate. They stayed out of sight, and took notes constantly.

He added, "My own ship, the *Eunice R.*, awaits me at Vera Cruz, where we land. Now my staff and I go above to look, listen, and learn. After seamen swab the decks each day, our seamice put chairs on the main deck for our own passengers, under the lifeboats, near the rail. There you'll enjoy the true beauty of life at sea."

So began the first of those unforgettable days.

Settled in deck chairs, we stared at the sunlit sea, the pale blue sky, the floating clouds as fluffy as whipped cream cheese. Overhead hung a large lifeboat that shaded us. In the distance whales spouted water, and porpoises played.

17

At tea-time stewards served cheese pastries.
Mornings were set aside for Spanish lessons, afternoons for lively discussions
between Basil and Marlane, which I found
most interesting.

They spoke of many things—pride and pro-
priety, snobs and society; chocolate and
cheeses, bridges and breezes; ghosts and geog-

18

raphy, pigs and photography; music and mystery, humans and history; sailors and scenery, mice and machinery.

Basil usually won those little wars of words, but Marlane was a worthy opponent, and one day he said admiringly, "For a female you are extremely intelligent, the equal of most males."

She stamped her foot angrily. "*Et tu,* Basil? You meant to compliment me, but I'm tired of being declared an honorary male. Judge us on our own, as doers, as achievers, as individuals!"

"*Bravo!*" I cried. "Here's to female rights! Fatherhood doesn't keep males from their careers. Motherhood's a noble role, but shouldn't mothers have careers, too? Even in this modern year of 1894, it's difficult! Some human females have succeeded—Dr. Elizabeth Blackwell, Nurse Florence Nightingale, who improved hospitals, Clara Barton, founder of the American Red Cross, and Marie Curie, gifted Polish scientist."

Marlane smiled. "The author of *Frankenstein* was Mary Shelley. The Brontë sisters

both wrote books, as did George Sand and George Eliot, women using men's names. There's Elizabeth Browning, poet, brilliant Judge Shirley Rose, Belva Lockwood, lawyer, Journalist Nellie Bly, who went around the world in seventy-two days. And what of our good and gracious Queen Victoria?"

She paced the deck. "Cécile Chaminade, composer, Suzanne Valadon, painter, Nellie Melba and Irene Adler, opera singers."

"I know of no female sleuths," declared Basil, "but Anna Katharine Green writes fine mysteries. So much for human females. Among mice, we'll always bless the Bedouin mousewife who, centuries ago, discovered the

20

curd from which cheese was first made. She is the most honored mouse in all history!''

Marlane dabbed at her eyes. ''Yet we are still second-class citizens, for we are denied the right to vote. It just doesn't seem fair!''

''Cheer up!'' said Basil. ''I predict that British females, both mouse *and* human, will win the vote in about twenty-five years, the Americans a little later. But Mexican female mice will vote long before any of them, because *you*, Marlane, are their apt and able champion!''

''I hope you've predicted correctly,'' she replied. ''And now, Basil, it's time that I revealed the secret of your mission to Mexico.''

The detective leaned forward, eyes agleam.

''Can the secret be—the theft of that priceless painting, the *Mousa Lisa?*''

Her eyes went wide with surprise. ''How on earth did you find out? Basil, you're a magician!''

4

The Theft of the Mousa Lisa

Basil leaned back in his deck chair, smiling. "My dear Marlane, magic had nothing to do with it. Last night I lay awake in my cabin, wondering what extraordinary event would make your government send halfway across the world for a detective. Ever since the cruel dictator, *El Bruto,* was exiled, Mexican mice have fared well under Novato, a wise and just president, and the crime rate is lower than ever before. However, the talk of the art world this past year was your country's purchase of

23

a great work of art, the *Mousa Lisa*. An enormous amount of money was paid for the masterpiece—or should I say *mousterpiece?*

"I pondered the problem, eliminated the impossible, and deduced as follows: first, that the painting had been stolen; second, that Mexico chose to keep the theft secret, for reasons unknown; third, that a fake must now hang in your museum."

Marlane sighed. "Your deductions are correct. But for the keen eyes of Jostes, an American artist, we'd still believe we had the original. Only Jostes and a few highly placed mice know of the fake, and all are sworn to secrecy."

I recalled the painting's history. In 1506 it had won instant fame for an unknown Italian, De Virgilio. Mousa Lisa, the beautiful niece

of a mouse duke, had posed for the portrait. The artist, who took two years to paint it, fell madly in love with his model. To keep her smiling he hired violinists to stroll around the studio, playing romantic music. Vases of flowers filled the air with fragrance. On the day the painting was unveiled he wed his adored Mousa Lisa.

A critic once wrote of the painting, "To see it is to feel one views a living, breathing being! How does one describe such matchless beauty? Golden brown fur, an oval face, eyes of shining innocence, and a smile so hauntingly lovely that long after leaving one yearns to return. For centuries mice have wondered about that smile, but none can agree on its meaning."

Basil's voice roused me from my reverie.

"The facts, Marlane, if you please."

"Very well, Basil. Before we bought the *Mousa Lisa,* Italy sometimes sent it out on loan. In Mexico it proved an absolute sensation! Señor Godoy, our museum curator, received thousands of letters suggesting that our government buy it. He wrote to Italy, asking

the price. At that time floods had damaged the Italian museum so badly that it needed to be rebuilt. Desperate for funds, the Italian mice quoted the unheard-of sum of one million Mexican pesos!

"We thought that would end the matter, but

every mouse in Mexico loved the painting, and each contributed. The poor gave one peso each, the rich gave thousands! Godoy, greatly loved by all, gave half his vast fortune, and urged friends to do likewise. He always helps poor artists. Our museum building, with all its works of art, was his generous gift to our country. He was sent to Italy for the painting. Upon his return, a holiday was declared. Mice from all over Mexico came to the capital to gaze at their *Mousa Lisa*."

Marlane paused. "We also have exhibits by living artists, such as the one-mouse show earlier this year by Jostes, an American. Diego and I met him the night he arrived. He said that as an art student in Italy he'd spent hours each day in front of the *Mousa Lisa*, studying De Virgilio's technique. This had helped his own style.

" 'May I visit the *Mousa Lisa* tonight, for old times' sake?' he asked. 'It's late, but surely the guards will admit President Novato.'

"Diego agreed. At first Jostes stood entranced, but then a terrible scowl darkened his

28

face, and he leaned over to peer closer at the painting.

"In a tragic voice he cried, 'F A K E !!!'

" 'Impossible!' declared Diego in disbelief.

" 'My hobby is detecting fakes,' replied Jostes. 'This is the best I've seen! I invented a scientific device that tells the true age of a work.'

"From his pocket he took an object the size of a watch, drew it slowly across the entire canvas. We waited in suspense. At last he said that the portrait, and even the cracks that made

it seem centuries old, had been done about a year ago, and then artificially aged. The million pesos had paid for a first-class fake!

"Our museum directors kept the news from the public, afraid there might be riots if the terrible truth were known. Jostes said that sometimes one who steals a masterpiece repents, and returns it without revealing his name. We waited two months, but in vain, and summoned you."

Basil rose. "Rest assured," he said resolutely, "that in Mexico I'll do all in my power to solve the mystery. Knowing Spanish will help greatly, Marlane—on with the lessons!"

So back we went to learning a lovely language—*comprar*, to buy, *volar*, to fly, *llorar*, to cry; *mandar*, to send, *prestar*, to lend, *terminar*, to end—to end this chapter, if you please.

5

Mexico the Magnificent

On a starry night we docked at the picturesque port of Vera Cruz, Mexico. Back in 1519 Spanish ships had put Cortez and his men ashore. Now, in 1895, we stole ashore, as quiet as mice.

Tall, handsome Vera Cruzan mice met us, and led us to a fiesta. Folk dancers in colorful costumes swirled and whirled about, and strolling mariachi bands played music from every state in Mexico.

Nibbling tacos, tortillas, and cheese enchila-

das, we watched the exciting Mexican Hat Dance. A big sombrero was placed on the floor. A male and female circled it, dancing on and off the brim so lightly that the hat never moved.

Marlane pulled Basil out on the floor, and the scientific sleuth surprised us—with his long Inverness cape flapping at his heels, he pranced and danced as nimbly as any Mexican!

We all kicked up our heels 'til the wee hours.

At dawn Marlane, Basil, and I were stowaways in an empty compartment on a people's train bound for Mexico City. We had thought to sleep, but the tropical scenery held us spellbound.

Spanish-style homes with red-tiled roofs were set on hillsides amid masses of exotic blooms. Slender palm trees swayed gently in the breeze. To the north loomed the snowy peaks of majestic Mount Orizaba, tallest in the land.

The train climbed slowly. Vera Cruz is at sea level, while Mexico City, on a plateau circled by mountains, is 7,415 feet high.

At journey's end, in the train station, we met President Diego Novato, who fondly embraced his long-absent wife. We liked him on sight.

He led us through the people's capital, ever on guard against huge human feet. Basil noted

that Mexican men had smaller feet than Englishmen, a great advantage from a mouse's-eye-view.

"Now we enter Chapultepec Park," declared Diego. "Our mouse capital is in the farthest corner, deep in the woods, safe from prying people."

The hidden city harmoniously blended European elegance and Mexican vitality. Our hotel was on Panadero Street near Plaza del Quesos.

After asking us to be at the museum at ten the next morning, Diego and Marlane departed.

Up in our suite of rooms I prepared for bed.

Basil, who'd been looking out of the window, turned around, eyes twinkling merrily.

"My dear doctor, I've just deduced that we won't be homesick in this hotel."

I slid under the blankets. "Why not, Basil?"

"The hotel happens to be on Panadero Street. *Panadero* is the Spanish word for *baker*. How could we ever be homesick on Baker Street?"

I snored loudly, pretending I hadn't heard.

6

The Investigation

We entered the museum early, and Luis Godoy, the frail, elderly curator, showed us through. The collection was the equal of any in Europe, with objects of art from every land —paintings, vases, statues, ancient carvings, exquisite jade.

Then he showed us the *Mousa Lisa* forgery that had deceived the experts.

"We put velvet ropes around it," he explained, "so that no one could come too close."

At ten, in Godoy's spacious office, we met the museum staff, from directors down to workmice.

The president spoke. "Fellow mice, the secret I am about to reveal must not be mentioned outside of this room. Our beloved *Mousa Lisa* has been stolen, and a copy hangs in its place!"

Shocked, they all began talking at once.

"Where is our *Mousa Lisa?*"

"Surely *El Presidente* is joking!"

"Who has committed this monstrous crime?"

"The thief should go to prison for life!"

The president held up his paw for silence.

"Permit me to introduce Basil of Baker Street, the Sherlock Holmes of the Mouse World!"

Basil bowed. "I promise to work day and night, if need be, to recover the missing masterpiece. First I must question each of you separately."

"Feel free to use my desk," remarked Godoy.

An envelope fell to the floor as Basil seated himself. Glancing at it, he passed it to Godoy, who also looked at it.

"From my doctor. A bill, no doubt. Basil, one of the workmice must leave early—his wife is ill. Will you question him first, *por favor?*"

My friend nodded. Everyone filed out of the room, except for a nervous mouse named Pablo.

"Señor Basil, I've worked here many years, and I'm told the job is mine for life. But a great detective such as you finds out everything, so I must confess my past. I did not steal the *Mousa Lisa*, but a long time ago I committed a crime. I was an innocent country mouse, new to the city. My friends were the wrong kind. They dared me to steal a watch. I was caught, and sent to jail. The museum doesn't know this. My wife knows, but not

my children. They would be *so* ashamed of their Papa! I beg you to keep my past a secret!"

Basil questioned him briefly, then said, "Go now, Pablo. I believe you to be an honest, hardworking mouse. Your secret is safe with me."

Pablo walked out proudly, his head held high.

A member of the Board of Directors next entered.

"Señor Saldaña, an emergency meeting was called when Jostes discovered the fake. Who attended?"

"The President and his lady, the artist Jostes, the curator, the other directors, and myself."

"How long did the meeting last?"

"Three hours. Everyone made suggestions."

"What were they, Señor Saldaña?"

"Some wanted to keep the news from the public, others wanted to tell, and offer a huge reward to get the painting back. Some wished to send for a famous French detective, others favored you. Still others said that the Mexican policemice should take complete charge of the case."

"Who suggested the Mexican policemice?"

"Two of the directors, and Godoy. I preferred you, Basil, as did Jostes, but he asked us to wait a month or two."

"I know why you waited," said the sleuth. "A great work of art can change a mouse's thinking. The *Mousa Lisa* was stolen once before, in Italy. The robber returned it, with a note saying he'd reformed. I understand your delay, but it makes matters difficult, for the trail is stone cold!"

"True. In the letter we sent you by messenger, we dared not mention the *Mousa Lisa*. Had Mexican mice learned of their loss, the entire nation would have been panic-stricken."

"What made you so sure I'd take the case?"

"We knew you'd deduce what had happened, and felt you couldn't resist the challenge."

Basil grinned. "Correct. By the by, do any of the museum mice paint professionally?"

"Some dabble at it, but not very successfully."

"I'll need a list of their names. Now—did any incident at the meeting strike you as unusual?"

"Yes indeed! When I opened the door, a file clerk fell headlong into the room. Obviously she'd been listening at the keyhole.

43

She denied it, said she was just passing by. We felt she lied, so we decided to tell her of the missing masterpiece and pledge her to secrecy."

Basil frowned. "Hmmm. Send her in, please."

Pilár was pretty, but her eyes were foxy. Basil asked whether she'd listened that day.

"*Si*, Señor Basil, but I lied about it. They were all so upset when they came to the meeting that I eavesdropped, out of curiosity."

"If curiosity killed a cat, it could also kill a mouse," stated Basil sternly. "Be warned!"

He questioned Pilár further, then dismissed her.

As the door closed he remarked, "A sly minx, if ever I saw one! Was it mere curiosity? Or was she in league with the crooks, under orders to report what went on? She's one of my suspects."

"How many do you have?" I inquired.

"You'll know in due time, Dawson."

The curator was next questioned.

"As you know, Basil, I sailed for Italy to

buy the *Mousa Lisa*. The crated painting stayed in my cabin the entire return voyage. No one entered except myself. At Vera Cruz, four armed guards waited to escort me to the capital, and directly to the museum. The guards then uncrated the painting, which we hung on the wall at once.''

"Señor Godoy, after you landed, could anyone have substituted a copy for the original?''

"No. The crate was never out of our sight.''

"That will be all, thank you," said Basil.

Mouse after mouse entered, and the questioning was not completed until well past noon.

Diego entered, saying, "Juan Romano, a guard who escorted Godoy from Vera Cruz, is in Merced Hospital with a broken leg. Do you wish to see him?''

Basil chuckled. "Most certainly. It will be a pleasure to meet a mouse named after a cheese.''

Romano, his leg in a cast, was sitting up in bed. Basil asked him to tell how the *Mousa Lisa* had been protected from dock to museum. The guard's story was exactly the same as Godoy's.

Romano's doctor came by, and I said in surprise, "Dr. Vega! We met at a London medical conference."

"Dawson! What brings you to Mexico?"

"I accompanied a famous friend, Basil of Baker Street," I replied, and introduced the two.

"May we meet for dinner?" asked Vega.

"After I solve my case, thank you," said Basil.

Vega gave me his card. Leaving the hospital, we headed back to our hotel.

7

The Panadero Street
Irregulars

Some shabbily dressed young mice were
playing ball on Panadero Street, outside the
hotel. The ball came our way, and Basil
tossed it back.

The youngster who caught it stared at the
sleuth.

"Señor, is it possible that you are Basil of
Baker Street? Himself? In the flesh? In per-
son?"

Basil's eyes were mischievous. "My dear
mouse, I must admit I'm not Sherlock
Holmes."

Wild with joy, the lads waved pieces of paper at him, begging for his autograph. Plainly, Basil was pleased, for he grinned like a Cheshire cat.

After signing seven little scraps of paper, he smiled down into seven dirty little faces.

"Do join us for lunch at the hotel," he said.

"We'd be delighted," I added, for a more lean and hungry-looking band I've seldom seen.

"But we are street *muchachos*," said one. "For such a fancy hotel, our clothes are old and worn and tattered and torn, and we own no others."

"No matter," answered Basil. "You shall be our honored guests. Come along, lads!"

Trailed by the raggle-taggle tribe, we entered the marble lobby, and then the dining room, ignoring the raised eyebrows of the other guests.

The headwaiter looked shocked. "But Señor—these street *muchachos* are not—are not—"

"Not welcome?" asked Basil. "On the contrary—we invited them. Kindly seat us at once."

The chairs were red velvet, the table was set with softly gleaming silver. The room was in

Spanish colonial style, with sparkling crystal chandeliers hanging from a high, arched ceiling. The lad who'd first spoken introduced the rest. "To my right, Ricardo, Edouardo, Bernardo. To my left, Roberto, Alberto, Gilberto. I'm Hector, the only one whose name doesn't rhyme, so they made me their leader. When do we eat, please?"

"At once. Order anything you like."

Seven smiles lit seven faces as they scanned the menu. What a love for cheese those mice had!

They ordered soup (sprinkled with grated cheese), *Chile Poblano* (stuffed with cheese), baked potato (with melted cheese), stewed cactus (with cheese sauce), and avocado salad (with cheese dressing).

What gigantic appetites! We watched them gobble up two and three portions of everything.

Even the headwaiter was amazed, and said, "If you've room for dessert, I suggest the strawberry cheesecake, popular among mice of the U.S.A."

We had one slice each, our guests had three!

"Certain lads in London," remarked Basil, "run errands and bring information to Sherlock Holmes. He calls them his Baker Street Irregulars. Will you seven lads be my Panadero Street Irregulars?"

"Si, si, si!" came the joyful chorus.

"So be it! Now, Dawson, I'd like Dr.

Vega's card. I wish to consult him at his office.''

I felt as though I'd been slapped. "But I've been your personal physician for years, Basil. Just tell me what the trouble is, and I'll have you fit as a fiddle in no time."

"I'd rather see Vega," he coldly replied.

So much for friendship, thought I, bitterly hurt. Too proud to plead, I passed over the card without another word.

Then he grinned. "Cheer up, friend! I'm seeing Vega about the case, not about my health."

"Harrumph. You might have said so," I grumbled.

"What will our first job be?" asked Hector.

"My dear Irregulars, I'm not familiar with your city," said Basil. "You're to guide me to Dr. Vega's office, and to a few other places. Also, I've heard of a dartboard with a cat's face painted upon it. I'd like Dr. Dawson to buy one for me. Do you know where they are sold, Hector?"

"On the Avenida de los Gatos. Ricardo, Edouardo, Bernardo, guide the good doctor there. Alberto, Roberto, Gilberto, come with Señor Basil and myself.''

Luckily, no cats prowled the Avenida de los Gatos. (*Gatos* is Spanish for *cats*.) In a quaint shop we found the painted dartboards. The cat faces were life-size, and looked all too real.

Ricardo whispered that in Mexico, those who pay the first price asked are considered half-witted, so I haggled in friendly fashion and paid far less than the original price.

Then I purchased another dartboard, as a gift for the young Irregulars. They kept thanking me all the long way back to the hotel.

Mr. Sherlock Holmes pays his Irregulars with a handful of English shillings. I paid ours with a pawful of Mexican pesos.

8

Who Was in the Attic?

Basil returned at dusk, and flung himself into an easy chair, long legs outstretched before him.

"Dawson, I had the devil of a time getting the medical history of a suspect from Dr. Vega. I finally told him about the *Mousa Lisa*, said that the data I sought would give me an important clue in the case. He then obliged me, and the trail is no longer cold, but red-hot! As for the suspect, you and I will visit him late tonight."

"*Him?* Then Pilár is not the guilty one."

"Pilár? Bah! She hasn't the brains of a cat!"

"Speaking of cats," I remarked, "just cast your eyes upon yonder wall."

He turned, and saw the dartboard. "Splendid!"

He picked up a dart, took his stance. Narrowing his eyes, he hurled the dart, which landed on the cat's chin. Swiftly he sent another flying, to pierce the painted pink nose.

"*Bravo!*" I cried. "Aim for those green eyes!"

He did, with happy results. Dozens of darts later he stopped, smiling contentedly.

"Having properly punished that ferocious feline," he said, "I am in the most mellow of moods. Frankly, if I weren't a mouse, I would purr."

"Because of your purr-fect score?" I joked, and dodged the pillow he threw.

After dinner we went upstairs for a game of chess. I must have dozed off, for Basil's voice roused me.

"Midnight, time to be on our way. You've been taking a catnap. If cats slept longer instead of catnapping, they'd have less time left for hunting mice."

We went forth, strolling along broad boulevards, past stately homes set on smooth, sloping lawns.

Basil halted before a tall, wrought-iron gate.

"Quickly, up and over before we're seen."

I obeyed. It was as though I'd entered an enchanted garden. There were splashing fountains, marble statues, beds of beautiful flowers.

The dwelling was in darkness, save for a small square of light high in an attic window.

Basil eyed a thin branch near that window.

"It will probably snap under my weight, but I'm afraid I'll have to go out on that limb. One strong gust of wind, and—"

"And down will come detective, deer-stalker, and all!" said I.

"Precisely. Still, I must chance it. Pray do not ask why. Soon you'll not only know why, but also who, what, where, when, and how."

We scurried up into the tree. Basil told me to stay near the trunk. Slowly he inched his way to the very end of the scraggly branch.

Then he leaned over to peer into the window.

I waited, wondering who was in the attic. I knew it wasn't Pilár, the foxy-eyed file clerk. Could it be Director Saldaña, or another director? Curator Godoy? Romano, who might have been released from the hospital? Or, if Basil had made an error in judgment, Pablo, who'd served a term in prison? Who, I asked myself, was in the attic?

At that moment there was a strong gust of wind. I hugged the tree trunk, just in time to keep from being blown away.

Not so fortunate was Basil, out on the limb. He went crashing down into a bird's nest!

I scurried below. "Any broken bones, Basil?"

"None. Luckily, the birds, who'd much rather eat mice than greet mice, are not at home. Look, Dawson—the light in the attic just went out!"

A muffled voice called, "I've been expecting you, Basil. Please go to the front entrance."

We descended, brushing bits of straw from our clothes, and mounted the marble steps.

The heavy oaken door swung slowly open.

"I bid you welcome," said Señor Godoy softly, and ushered us inside.

9

A Strange Story

We followed the frail, elderly curator through the vast entrance hall into his book-lined study.

"*Por favor*, be seated," he said. "The servants are asleep, else I'd ring for refreshment."

"It is not for refreshment that we came," said Basil, "but for your story. Will you begin?"

The curator's strange story was made even more strange by his courtly, formal way of speaking.

"Know that I, Luis Ernesto Felipe de Godoy, am descended from a long line of Spanish noblemice. My ancestors came to Mexico with Cortez in 1519. I am the last of my line, never having married.

"I was sent to Italy to buy the *Mousa Lisa*. As soon as I arrived I went to the museum. I had seen many masterpieces, but never this one, and its effect upon me was unbelievable! The moment I saw that fabulous face, that haunting smile, I was bewitched, as though a spell had been cast over me. From then on I was a changed mouse. I knew I'd lie or forge or steal, if need be, to possess the painting. Share her beautiful image with others? Never! The *Mousa Lisa* had to be mine, and mine alone!"

A tear trickled down his wrinkled cheek.

"As a youth one summer in Spain I'd studied painting privately. My teacher said I'd never be a great artist, or even a fair one, but he praised my skill as a copyist. I stopped my studies, began helping poor young artists with real talent, and became a leading art expert.

"Standing there in the Italian museum before the *Mousa Lisa*, I resolved to make a copy for the Mexican mice, and keep the original for myself.

"I went to the director's office, paid him the million pesos, and was told that the next night, when my ship sailed, armed guards would bring the painting aboard, packed in a crate to protect it.

"I asked what it measured minus the frame, and memorized the exact figures. That evening there was a reception at the museum in my honor.

"The next day, my last in Italy, was a busy one. As an expert, I'd often judged whether a work was original or faked. Forgers would use paints from tubes to create a fake, and claim it was centuries old, not knowing that painters of long ago ground their own colors. I paid an Italian mouse artist well to grind certain colors and put them in jars. Next I bought brushes, canvases, a folding easel, a book on forgery, and a suitcase. In a park I scooped dirt into a small box, and put everything into the suitcase.

"That night guards brought the crate

aboard. I told Captain Ryder I'd remain in my cabin during the voyage, and wished my meals left on a tray outside my door. I asked that no stewards enter the cabin, because of the painting. He agreed.

"I locked my door, and spent the night reading *Memoirs of an Art Forger,* written in prison by a Dutch mouse. I'd sent him there by exposing him as a forger—now I was one myself.

"Early next morning I uncrated the painting and placed it on the easel, facing me. I sat at the desk and sketched the eyes, not once, not

ten times, but hundreds of times! I drew eyes until my own eyes grew weary, and I slept.

"The following day I did noses, imitating De Virgilio's style closely. I spent several days on lips, shoulders, paws, fur, gown, and so on. I forged the signature, over and over."

Godoy paused. Somewhere a clock chimed three.

"A week later I began painting on canvases that were the same size as the original, and did ten copies. I aged the best one by making tiny cracks in the canvas, rubbing dirt into the cracks. I aged the wooden stretchers that held the canvas.

"Next to the true *Mousa Lisa,* my copy, although perfect, lacked a certain glow. Still, if I, the great art expert, said it was the original, who would doubt my word? I removed the frame from the original and framed the fake, which I crated. Then I rolled up the real painting.

"Putting everything I'd used into the suitcase, I heaved it overboard at midnight. Thus did I dispose of all clues. Two days later we landed.

"At Vera Cruz, the museum guards who met me patted the crate fondly, little dreaming that beneath my long, black cloak was the real *Mousa Lisa*, rolled up and strapped to my side."

The curator sighed heavily, and rose.

"My friends, I shall show her to you now."

He led the way to the attic, where he

pressed against a panel. The entire wall swung outward, revealing a secret room.

There, on an easel, was the greatest masterpiece of the mouse world—the real *Mousa Lisa!*

10
Basil's Decision

The portrait had a warm, rich glow, a vivid loveliness that leaped from the canvas to dazzle the eye of the beholder. Like a mouse goddess of old, the real *Mousa Lisa* was divinely beautiful!

Godoy sank into a chair, weary beyond words.

"Here I spend my spare moments, Basil. But of late her eyes seem to reproach me, to accuse me of robbing and deceiving my fellow-mice. Had you not found me out, I'd soon have confessed my crime, for it haunts me night and day. Living without honor is too heavy a burden to bear.''

''I suspected you from the start,'' said Basil, ''but I held back, knowing you to be the best-loved mouse in all Mexico, with a lifetime of service to others. I concentrated on other suspects, even on Pablo, in whose innocence I firmly believed. In their neighborhoods I chatted with their families and friends, soon deducing that not Romano or Pilár or Pablo was clever enough to have planned and executed the theft.''

Paws clasped behind him, Basil paced the room.

''Certain questions could not be ignored. How many mice were involved? Was the crime the work of known art thieves, or amateurs? Who had painted the fake, and when, and where? My thoughts turned to Saldaña and yourself, both apparently above suspicion. What had gone on in your cabin during the long sea voyage? I had a theory, but could not prove it.

''Then Saldaña, on being questioned, said

70

you'd suggested putting the Mexican policemice on the case, rather than sending for me,
and I was forced to conclude that you were
guilty. You see, of all Mexican mice, you are
the most widely traveled, and would be well
aware of my international fame as a sleuth.
Mexican policemice are capable, but there's
not one famous detective among them. Why,
then, would you prefer them to myself?''

The curator bowed his head. ''Because you
alone are brilliant enough to ferret out the
truth.''

''Precisely. But why does a mouse of honor
turn to crime? For money? I made inquiries.
You were, and are, very rich. Was it a passion
to possess De Virgilio's greatest work? I felt
there was a stronger reason. At the museum,
when an envelope addressed to you fell from
your desk, I saw the name of the sender, Dr.
Vega. By chance we ran into him at Merced
Hospital. Later I went to his office to discuss
the state of your health.''

The curator's voice trembled. ''Then you
know? I want no pity! I asked Dr. Vega to tell
no one.''

Basil said kindly, "He betrayed your secret only when I said the *Mousa Lisa* had been stolen, and the information might help me solve the case. When I learned you had a rare, incurable disease, and but a short time to live, all was crystal clear. You stole the painting so that its radiant beauty would enrich the last few months of your life."

Basil then mentioned the disease, and I nodded. It was indeed incurable, but at least this gentle soul would suffer no physical pain.

Godoy, his face haggard, looked at Basil.

"Disgrace and imprisonment are what I deserve. Do you require a written confession?"

Tears rushed to his eyes, and I brushed away a tear or two of my own. What would Basil do?

What he did proved again that he was the best and wisest mouse I'd ever known, that beneath his stern exterior beat a heart of purest gold.

Patting Godoy's shoulder, he said, "No need to write that confession. One misstep does not erase a life of unselfish service to others. None but ourselves will know what you did. You'll still be first in the hearts of your countrymice, now and always! I'll tell the museum directors that the painting was returned to me with no clues as to the thief's identity, and that I now consider the case closed. Señor, I venture to predict joy so great that no questions will be asked."

Godoy led us down to the kitchen, where he wrapped the painting in plain brown paper.

"Bless you, Basil," he called out as we

left. "And you as well, Dr. Dawson—bless you both!"

As we walked through the gardens, I re-marked, "Thanks to your kind heart, Basil, he'll spend his last days here, amidst beautiful things, instead of in an ugly jail cell."

But Basil, who had had his fill of praise that day, said lightly, "Speaking of jail, what's the difference between a jailer and a jeweler?"

"I've no idea, Basil—what *is* the difference?"

"Elementary, my dear doctor! A jeweler sells watches and a jailer watches cells."

I groaned in mock reproof, and we returned to the hotel to catch up on much-needed sleep.

Late that morning there was a special meeting at the museum. As Basil had predicted, all were so overjoyed at the recovery of the masterpiece that they accepted the explanation without any questions. Congratulating him, they crowded around to gaze in rapture at the painting.

Godoy, who looked rested and in good spirits, had the museum closed to visitors for an hour. We watched as he hung the real *Mousa Lisa* where she rightfully belonged, at long last!

President Novato took Basil aside, declaring, "Well done! I'm positive that your presence in Mexico influenced the thief to return the painting. Name any fee you wish—the sky's the limit!''

"Diego, my fee is a modest one. First, instead of paying me, have your government set aside funds for college educations for seven clever young mice—my Panadero Street Irregulars. And second, as a memento of this unusual case, I'd like that marvelous *Mousa Lisa* fake shipped to my lodgings at Baker Street, Number 221,B. Is that agreeable?''

"Perfectly. Both requests will be granted and you have our undying gratitude. By the way, our policemice, who admire you vastly, have asked that you address them tomorrow morning, on any topic you choose. Will you oblige them?''

Basil agreed, and we left. At the hotel messages from friends in the International Society of Mouse Mountaineers awaited us. They'd come to climb Mount Popocatépetl. We belonged to the ISMM, and decided to make the climb.

I left a note saying we'd see them at dinner. That evening we entered the dining room for a happy reunion with old friends—Lord Adrian, the Maharajah of Bengistan, Young Richard, Vincenzo Starretti, Frank Reilly, Dr. Julian Wolff, and others, including Luther Norris, a bookseller specializing in mysteries, who lived in Mexico.

He bore gifts—a Sherlockian story translated into Greek for Basil, another in Latin for me, and three Basil of Baker Street tales in Spanish.

We thanked the thoughtful bookmouse, and then began to discuss the Mt. Popocatépetl climb.

"I've climbed Popo twice," said Luther. "If you like, I'll guide you. Carmencita, a friendly burro, can transport you with supplies and equipment. If you wish me to see her tomorrow about arrangements, I'll be glad to do so."

We voted for his proposal, after which we sampled an impressive array of Mexican cheeses, as though we hadn't a care in the world.

But alas for the plans of mice and men—at

that very moment evildoers were hatching a sinister plot! Had the merrymakers at our table known what lay ahead, they would have been plunged into deepest gloom.

11
Dr. Dawson Disappears!

It is with a heavy heart that I, Basil of Baker Street, take pen in paw to write these lines.

Would that Dawson were here to do so— alas, he has disappeared, I know not where! But let me recount today's events as they occurred.

This morning I addressed the Mexican policemice. Title of my talk: "The Detection and Analysis of Pawprints." Dawson has heard me on this topic many times before, so I left without waking him.

My speech was well received, and later I was guest of honor at a luncheon, seated between General Sierra and Police Chief Garcia. At the end of the luncheon, Sierra mentioned that the entire mouse army, except for the palace guard, was on maneuvers in Cuernavaca, about fifty miles away.

"Do you mean to say that you leave your capital unguarded?" I asked in surprise.

"We're at peace, Basil," answered General Sierra. "With *El Bruto,* the cruel tyrant who once ruled us, under heavy guard on the faraway island to which we exiled him, there is nothing to fear."

"How true!" said Police Chief Garcia. "For five days, all over Mexico, not a single crime has been committed. Doesn't that convince you, Basil?"

I frowned. "On the contrary! The complete absence of crime indicates that all gangs have joined forces. I fear something big is brewing! Both police and army should be alerted, ready to move."

Chief Garcia patted my shoulder. "Your

fame is worldwide, but in this case you are mistaken.''

We parted, and I headed for the hotel, where I found a note from Dawson, written that morning. A messenger had come with word of an English noblemouse lying ill of a fever at the Hotel Elegante. Dawson had gone there, and hoped to be back soon.

He's late, I told myself, for it was already midafternoon. I busied myself writing a monograph entitled *The Hunting Habits of Tomcats*.

When darkness fell, with no sign of my friend, I grew alarmed, and resolved to investigate. I asked the Irregulars, playing outside, to lead me to the Elegante. The neighborhood worsened as we raced along, and we were soon deep in the slums.

The Hotel Elegante was the opposite of elegant. Shamefully rundown, with broken window panes and peeling paint, it stood on a narrow street that was littered with rubbish.

Telling the lads to remain outside, I entered.

A slovenly clerk slouched at the front desk.

I introduced myself, then said, *"Por favor,* I should like some information. Is there an English noblemouse registered at this hotel?"

He laughed in my face. "Since when do high-class mice stay at a dump like the Elegante?"

"Nevertheless," said I, "a doctor was summoned here to treat an English mouse reported to be ill."

The rude clerk yawned. "Well, maybe I *did* see a mouse with a doctor's bag go upstairs."

"Was he alone? Did you see him leave?"

"How should I know? I'm no watchdog!"

Just then Hector ran into the lobby.

"Señor Basil!" he called in great excitement. "An old corn-seller says he saw two mice leave the hotel earlier, and one carried a little black bag."

I dashed outside to meet the corn-seller, who was roasting corn over a small fire in his cart. I bought corn for us all, and nibbled as I listened.

"Señor, this morning I saw two mice leave the hotel. One had a doctor's bag. The other, whose face was evil, had his paw pressed against the doctor's back. I think he was holding a gun."

I stared at the old corn-seller, and suddenly everything clicked in my mind! My detective's instinct told me that once more I had come to grips with my old enemy, Professor Ratigan. I have a healthy respect for these hunches of mine, which have so often been proven correct.

"Tell me," said I, "was this other mouse thin, with a high, bony forehead, and deep-set piercing eyes? Was he unusually tall, about my height?"

The corn-seller's face was a study in surprise.

"Then you saw him, Señor? You describe him well."

"I did not see him today, but thanks to you, I now know that the leader of the mouse underworld has arrived in Mexico. Because I put a stop to his counterfeit cheese crimes in

London, he seeks revenge upon me through my friend Dr. Dawson.''

I turned to face the Panadero Street Irregulars.

''Lads, I'll go to the ends of the earth, if need be, to find my good friend and yours, Dr. David Q. Dawson. I'll track down that scoundrel Ratigan if it's the last thing I do!''

12
Ratigan's Revenge

Once again I confronted the cheeky clerk.

"You had better cooperate," I declared
sternly. "You rented a room to a tall, thin
English mouse who is a wanted criminal. He
left the hotel this morning. Unless you let
me inspect the room he occupied, I shall notify
the policemice at once."

Grudgingly the clerk produced a key. My
young companions and I dashed upstairs to
Room 23, and unlocked the door. The bed had
been stripped of linen, and the wastebasket

emptied, but luckily the floor had not yet been swept.

Whipping out my magnifying lens, I got down on all fours and circled the room. Not one square inch of the floor escaped my careful scrutiny, and at last I was rewarded—beneath the wastebasket were two small shreds of bright yellow paper.

I studied the tiny scraps, my only clues. Part of a word was written on each—*pri* and *aw*. What could they possibly signify?

Leaning against a bedpost, I concentrated on the words that went marching through my mind.

Of what word was *pri* a part? Price? Prize? Surprise? Private? Printing? Privilege? Or was the word—PRISONER?

Aw would be more difficult, for there were but two letters. From what word had it come? Paw? Claw? Straw? Crawl? Scrawl? Awful? Unlawful? Or perhaps—DAWSON?

Clearly, Dawson was a prisoner somewhere, and I was on the right track, but I needed more in the way of clues than those two scraps.

Out in the grimy hallway stood a large basket of trash. I called the maid, gave her a peso, and told her we had to rummage through the rubbish.

"Don't worry, Señora," I said, "my friends will dump it out, but they'll put it all back so there won't be any extra work for you."

The maid nodded, and shuffled down the hall.

I turned the trash basket upside down, and the lads and I began hunting for the bright yellow scraps.

Placing my deerstalker on the floor, I said, "Put every piece you find in here, so we'll know exactly where they all are."

What a quantity of trash we inspected! It seemed endless, and we sifted it again and again until our eyes ached. Finally I was convinced that we had found every last scrap of yellow paper, about a hundred in all.

I supervised the lads as they put the trash back in the trash basket. Then I picked up my deerstalker and carried our precious finds back to Room 23, where I laid them carefully on the desk.

"It's like a jigsaw puzzle," remarked Roberto.

"Correct! The most important jigsaw puzzle

on earth, for it is our only clue to the strange disappearance of Dr. Dawson. To work, Irregulars!''

Progress was maddeningly slow, for the paper had been torn to tiny shreds. Children are better at this sort of thing than adults, and I was glad of their patient persistence.

An hour later I read this disturbing message:

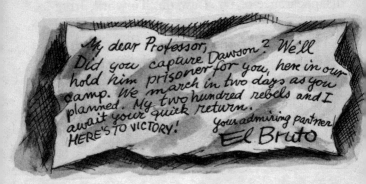

My dear Professor,
Did you capture Dawson? We'll
hold him prisoner for you, here in our
camp. We march in two days as you
planned. My two hundred rebels and I
await your quick return.
HERE'S TO VICTORY!   your admiring partner
El Bruto

My senses reeled! Ratigan must have arranged the dictator's escape from the island so
that cruel *El Bruto* could overthrow the government.

No wonder there'd been no crime for five
days—no doubt Ratigan had rounded up all
the Mexican mouse gangs, so his own gangmice could train them. With *El Bruto* back in
power, Ratigan would share in the profits as
the rascally pair ruthlessly robbed the unlucky
mice under their rule.

I had to act! Two hundred rebels could not
hide in the city without attracting attention, so
they had to be camped elsewhere.

I asked, "Is there a place not too far from the capital, one that would make a good hideaway?"

Bernardo nodded. "The Old Fort. It's crumbling to ruins, and nobody visits it anymore."

"Except for Basil of Baker Street, who will go there in disguise," I declared, striding downstairs, the lads at my heels.

Outside I told the corn-seller I'd pay well for the use of his cart the next day, and he promised to bring it to my hotel at eight in the morning.

Back in the city, I sent the Irregulars home, after inviting them for breakfast the next day.

At a store where used clothes were sold, I bought attire like that of the corn-seller—a worn white shirt and trousers, scuffed leather sandals, and a battered old sombrero.

I tossed and turned all night, worrying about Dawson, and wondering whether the morrow would bring success or failure.

13

In the Camp of the Enemy

Rising early, I proceeded to disguise myself. Dawson often refers to me as a master in the art of disguise, and I must say I agree.

My theatrical makeup box holds many magical surprises. I'll not reveal my secrets, except to tell you that wads of cotton stuffed in my cheeks made my cheekbones prominent in a Mexican way. Other tricks created wrinkles and worrylines, adding years to my appearance. Working before my mirror, I soon transformed the sharp-eyed sleuth into a sleepy-eyed corn-seller.

The Irregulars waiting in the lobby failed to recognize me in the stooped old mouse who shuffled up to greet them in the corn-seller's voice.

Then, in regular tones, I said, "May I introduce the Sherlock Holmes of the Mouse World?"

Their astonishment proved how well I'd disguised myself, and we went in to breakfast.

Afterward, in an alley, the corn-seller acted as my teacher. He lit a small fire in his cart,

roasted an ear of corn and poured melted cheese over it. I watched closely, and practiced it many times, as did Hector. There was no problem in disposing of the roasted corn—the Irregulars gobbled them up.

I told Hector that he would accompany me to the Old Fort as my son. The others were disappointed, but did not complain. They knew I was engaged in a most perilous mission.

Wheeling the cart, I began the two-hour walk to the fort, Hector at my side. At ten-thirty we trod a grassy lane leading to the fort's entrance. Two sentries in faded uniforms stood at the rusty gates. They peered out suspiciously, but before they could order us to move on, I held up some corns.

"For you, *Soldados*, free, as many as you like! In return, I ask one small favor from two such handsome soldiers. Let me in to sell corn to your comrades. This is Hector, my Number One Son. Today is his birthday. With so many soldiers in your fort, my corn will soon be sold, and then I can go home to celebrate my sons's birthday."

As I spoke, I kept roasting more corn. The delicious smell was wafted to the guards' nostrils.

"*El Bruto* won't even know," said one guard to the other. "He's with Ratigan—they talk for hours."

They opened the gates and we entered. I gave them their free corn, then wheeled the cart further inside. At once the rebels crowded around—the heavenly smell of melting cheese was a temptation none could resist, and they kept us busy.

I was glad of my disguise, for I spotted some of Ratigan's gangsters. Among my customers were Doran, the Flashy Farrell Brothers, Lefty Lichina, and Sean Wright, known as Wrongo Wright.

"Carry on!" I whispered to Hector, who nodded, and I wormed my way through the crowd.

It was then that I saw the prison pen, enclosed by a high, chain-link fence. In it, head bowed and paws manacled, sat my friend Dawson.

Sidling over, I said softly, "My dear doctor, where is *El Bruto's* tent? I wish to eavesdrop."

He smiled. "I knew you'd find me! And what a perfect disguise! Go to the largest tent —the rebels are too busy nibbling corn to notice you. Ratigan and *El Bruto* are plotting something big, I believe. When will you act?"

"Early tomorrow, old friend. See you then!"

My pocketknife made a small slit in the

back of the tent, enabling me to see as well as hear. Inside was my most relentless foe, Professor Padraic Ratigan, Crown Prince of Crime! I saw *El Bruto*, too, a big brute of a mouse whose tiny pig-eyes glittered as he spoke.

"Ratigan, you're a wonder! Five days ago you arranged my escape from the island, even had a wax dummy of me fall into the sea so the guards would think sharks had devoured me. You rounded up my rebels, and all Mexican gangmice not in jail. Your confederate Doran, formerly of the Mouse Foreign Legion, trained them as soldiers. Professor, we can't fail, and you, my partner, will share the loot. Rob and rule, that's my motto! By the way, have you decided Dawson's fate yet?"

"More or less. He's a valuable hostage. I'll threaten to harm him if Basil tries to stop us. Basil, the only mouse whose brainpower

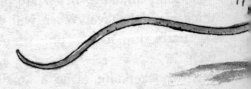

equals my own, is the one mouse I fear! He and I could rule the entire mouse world, be rich beyond belief. I've told him so, but the stubborn fool refuses to become my ally! We'll imprison his crony, Dawson, in the palace when we take over the government.''

El Bruto cried, "Tomorrow we triumph! Napoleon once said that an army marches on its stomach. At six in the morning my rebels will fill their bellies with breakfast. And at six-thirty we'll march on the capital!"

I had heard enough. As I darted away I looked up at a steep cliff just beyond the rear wall of the fort, and an idea formed in my mind.

Hector and I left. Once out of sight of the soldiers, I trained my spyglass on the cliff. Halfway up I glimpsed the mouth of a cave. I couldn't climb on this side, lest I be seen, but a path around the foot of the cliff led to the opposite side, away from the fort. We followed it.

Again using my spyglass, I saw there was also a cave on this side. Was there a connecting tunnel? I had to find out, and at once!

I said, "Hector, rush to the palace! Tell *El Presidente* I must speak to him and General Sierra later today on a life-and-death matter. Hurry!"

He scampered off, pushing the cart before him.

Straight up the cliff I went, and into the cave. It opened into a long tunnel, through which I went. As I'd hoped, the tunnel led to the cave on the enemy's side. I peeped out, studying the scene.

Far below lay the rebels' camp, and now I knew exactly what my strategy would be.

14

Attack Before Dawn

I raced back through the tunnel, descended the cliff, and hastened toward the capital as fast as my legs could carry me.

President Novato and General Sierra awaited me in a conference room of the palace.

"Contrary to any reports you may have heard," I said, *"El Bruto* is not reposing in the stomach of a shark. The cruel dictator is alive and well, determined to rule the mice of Mexico again, and plotting with Professor

Ratigan to overthrow the present government. They must be halted, and I strongly advise certain military tactics.

"To rout the rebels," I continued, "stage a surprise attack! Recall your troops from Cuernavaca at once. We'll meet them at midnight at the cliff, on the side away from the enemy camp. Half the soldiers, assisted by our experienced ISMM-ers, will ascend the cliff to the cave. A tunnel leads to another cave on the rebels' side, overlooking the Old Fort. We'll attack before dawn, and I myself shall lead them!

"Under General Sierra's command, the remaining troops will march around the foot of the cliff. As soon as my mice attack at the rear of the camp, the General's mice will gather at the front gates to prevent the enemy from escaping. Thus boxed in, *El Bruto's* mice will quickly surrender."

The General bowed. "My congratulations! It is exactly the strategy I'd have proposed. Basil, you're a military genius! Would you care to accept the rank of general in our Mexican mouse army?"

"You honor me," I replied, "but my only aim is to follow in the footsteps of Sherlock Holmes."

Orders were dispatched to the troops at once.

General Sierra and I, along with our mountain-climbing experts and their specialized equipment, reached the rendezvous at midnight.

The troops were already there, ready for action.

Led by General Sierra, half the company stole silently along the path circling the cliff.

The rest were under my command. Lord Adrian, Young Richard, and Bob Hahn climbed to the cave, fastened ropes there and dropped them down.

On the ground, guided by other ISMM-ers, the Mexicans grasped the ropes and made the difficult ascent, then scurried along the tunnel to the cave on the other side. Aware of the long wait ahead, I suggested that they snatch some sleep.

In a corner of the cave I paced to and fro, analyzing the final steps of my strategy.

Just before dawn I awakened my sleeping beauties, cautioning them to silence. The mountaineers proceeded to the ledges below, in order to help the soldiers down the almost perpendicular cliff. Everything went like clockwork. The unsuspecting rebels slept on. We reached the ground and inched forward in the tall grass.

We scaled the rear wall of the fort and crouched there, prepared to do or die. The crucial moment had come! My own breathing

was like thunder in my ears as I stood upright, signaling the others to do the same.

Now or never, I thought, and shouted, *"Adelante, Soldados!* CHARGE!!!"

The long line of troops leaped to the ground, screaming what I'd told them to scream.

"MIAOU!   MIAOU!   MIAOU!"

Their savage screeching shattered the stillness as they advanced, wildly waving their rifles.

Terror-stricken mice stumbled from their tents. trembling in every limb! They soon saw that the raiders were mice, but the cat-cries had robbed the rebels of the will to fight. Seeking to escape at the gates, they were met by Sierra's soldiers.

Stunned and bewildered, they surrendered. My surprise strategy had been a spectacular success!

El Bruto accepted his defeat, but Ratigan's eyes glared balefully as he faced me.

I glared back. "Vile villain! You'll stand trial in Mexico as kidnapper and conspirator, and serve a jail term. Then they'll deport you to England to answer for your other crimes."

"Don't count on it, Basil! We'll meet again, and when we do—watch out!"

He was led away, still muttering threats against me, while Dawson and I held a glad reunion.

The Mystery of the Doctor's Disappearance has been solved. Without further ado, I place my pen in Dawson's distinguished paws.

15

Northward to Arizona

With a bow to Basil, my able substitute, I resume the account of our Mexican adventures.

To celebrate the defeat of *El Bruto,* a cheese-tasting banquet was held at the palace. We met Sir John Hathaway, British Mouse Ambassador, and his wife, Lady Paula. Excellent cheese and excellent company made for a memorable evening.

At sunrise the next day we set out to climb Popo. Carmencita, a charming burro, waited outside the mouse capital, being too big to enter. We loaded our supplies and equipment, then mounted.

As she jogged along, we sometimes got glimpses of the mighty volcano, whose snow-capped summit seemed to be touching the clouds.

Carmencita left us at the foot of the volcano, promising to return in a week.

People and mice often climbed Popo, which hadn't erupted in years. The upper slopes were extremely cold, and we almost had a tragedy. Frank Reilly wandered off the trail and was lost in a swirling snowstorm for hours, but Luther Norris finally found him.

In the distance we could see Popo's mate, Mount Ixtacihuatl, called Ixta by the Mexicans. But one volcano was enough for us, and we were waiting down below when Carmencita returned.

Accompanying her was Pepito, her handsome young nephew, who'd come especially to meet Basil. The detective rewarded him by riding on his back and discussing his most exciting cases.

Along the way Pepito had a toothache. Dr. Wolff and I climbed up to peer into his mouth. The tooth was too badly decayed to be saved.

"Ever pull a burro's tooth?" Wolff asked me.

"No, Julian, but there's one method that never fails, for mice, for men, or for burros."

We tied one end of a rope around Pepito's tooth, while Carmencita held the other end in her mouth.

"It will be over in a minute," I told Pepito.

And to his aunt I said, "What's rope to a mouse is but string to a burro. STEP BACK!"

She did so, and out came the tooth. Wolff and I packed the cavity with gauze and antiseptic, and young Pepito was soon his smiling self again.

When Carmencita heard that we hoped to visit the United States soon, she volunteered to transport us to the border. We accepted her offer.

In the capital we learned that Señor Godoy had passed away. Thousands came to do him homage at his funeral, a fitting end for a fine mouse. Only Basil and I knew the secret he carried to his grave.

Our ISMM friends were staying on to climb Mount Orizaba, but Basil and I wanted to see Arizona's Grand Canyon, and the rest of the West. Hathaway mentioned a mouse hotel nearby, owned by their former cook and butler.

"Basil, they write that weird, mysterious happenings drive guests away. If forced to close, they'll lose their life savings."

"I'll look into the matter," replied Basil. " 'Twill sharpen my sleuthing skills."

When we left, many Mexican mice waved in farewell—the Panadero Street Irregulars, Marlane, Diego, and dozens of others.

As Carmencita jogged along, Basil said, "My dear doctor, there are wildcats in the Wild West. Do you think there are wildmice as well?"

I smiled mischievously. "My dear detective, curb your curiosity—you'll know in due time."

And, ignoring his annoyed squeals, I dozed off.

ABOUT THE AUTHOR
AND ILLUSTRATOR

EVE TITUS is the author of twenty children's books, including those about the French cheese-tasting mouse, Anatole. A professional concert pianist, she has always had two loves—writing and music. Miss Titus originated and personally conducts her Storybook Writing Seminar several times a year, and during the summer in Europe as a traveling workshop combined with a children's literature program. Because of Mouse Basil, Miss Titus is President of the Sherlock Holmes Society of Los Angeles. Born and raised in New York City, she lived for several years in Mexico and California. Italy is her present home, and summers are spent on a small Greek island, writing and giving her workshop. Of the first *Basil of Baker Street* mystery, Adrian M. Conan Doyle wrote the author, "May I offer you my heart-felt congratulations. It is a simply wonderful creation, and I can assure you that my father would have revelled in every page." Numerous Sherlockian collectors prize the *Basil of Baker Street* mysteries, which include *Basil of Baker Street, Basil and the Pygmy Cats,* and *Basil and the Lost Colony*, available in Archway Paperback editions.

PAUL GALDONE came to this country from Budapest, Hungary, and studied at the Art Students League in New York. He is a well-known illustrator of children's literature and lives with his wife and their two children in Rockland County, New York.